Alex opened the doors to the mall. "Come on." She grinned as she led T-Bone, her dog, inside.

Janie and Lorraine could not stop giggling. They followed Alex and T-Bone into the stream of people shopping in the mall.

"Hurry up," Alex called to them. "You need to walk on either side of T-Bone to help hide him."

"Oh, Alex!" Janie covered her face with her hands. "This is so embarrassing!"

Alex ignored the laughter and the stares of the people around them. She and the dog moved straight ahead as if it were the most natural thing in the world to bring a dog to a shopping mall.

"Uh oh, brussels sprouts!" Alex suddenly cried. "I see a policeman! . . . And he's coming this way."

## The ALEX Series
*by Nancy Simpson Levene*

- Shoelaces and Brussels Sprouts
- French Fry Forgiveness
- Hot Chocolate Friendship
- Peanut Butter and Jelly Secrets
- Mint Cookie Miracles
- Cherry Cola Champions
- The Salty Scarecrow Solution
- Peach Pit Popularity
- T-Bone Trouble
- Grapefruit Basket Upset
- Apple Turnover Treasure
- Crocodile Meatloaf
- Chocolate Chips and Trumpet Tricks
    —an Alex Devotional

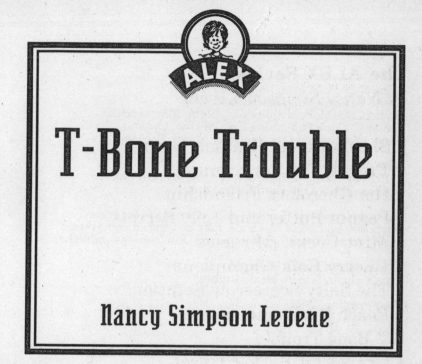

# ALEX

# T-Bone Trouble

## Nancy Simpson Levene

## Chariot Books™

Chariot Books™ is an imprint of
David C. Cook Publishing Co.
David C. Cook Publishing Co., Elgin, Illinois 60120
David C. Cook Publishing Co., Weston, Ontario
Nova Distribution Ltd., Newton Abbot, England

Cover design by Bill Paetzold
Cover illustration by Neal Hughes

First Printing, 1990
Printed in the United States of America
97 96 95 94 93  7 6 5 4

**Library of Congress Cataloging-in-Publication Data**
Levene, Nancy Simpson.
T-bone trouble/Nancy SImpson Levene; illustrated by
Susan Morris.
          p.cm.
Summary: When the new girl at school starts spreading lies
about her, Alex loses some friends and comes to a new
understanding of honesty, loyalty, and forgiveness.
ISBN 1-55513-765-2
[1. Honesty—Fiction. 2. Friendship—Fiction. 3.
Schools—Fiction. 4. Conduct of life—Fiction.] I. Morris,
Susan, ill. II. Title
PZ7.L5724Tac   1990                          90-32906
[Fic]—dc20                                   CIP  AC

# CONTENTS

1 Trouble Begins                          7
2 Ugly Gossip                            22
3 A Deadly Fall                          36
4 Hospital Prayers                       45
5 A Bathroom Fight                       57
6 Adventure with T-Bone                  69
7 Dog in the Mall                        80
8 T-Bone's Disaster                      95
9 Forgive Julie?                        108
10 Friends Again                        120

*To Jesus, our Lord,*
*Who is faithful to lead His sheep*
*Up the narrow path of His mountain*
*and*
*To my daughter, Cara, who is learning to*
*walk in the deep places of His path.*

*So it was that when they gave God up and*
*would not even acknowledge him, God gave them*
*up to doing everything their evil minds could*
*think of. Their lives became full of every kind of*
*wickedness and sin, of greed and hate, envy,*
*murder, fighting, lying, bitterness, and gossip.*
*Romans 1:28, 29*
*The Living Bible*

*Your heavenly Father will forgive you if you*
*forgive those who sin against you; but if you*
*refuse to forgive them, he will not forgive you.*
*Matthew 6:14, 15*
*The Living Bible*

## ACKNOWLEDGMENTS
I thank my mom and dad and Patti for their unfailing support and I thank Ed for his good ideas. Thank you, Greg, Maribeth, Miriam, and Marge, for being so interested in Alex.

# CHAPTER 1

## Trouble Begins

Alex stood silently in the middle of her bedroom floor. Had she heard someone call for help? Motioning for her friend Melissa to be quiet, Alex listened again. There was no doubt about it. A faint "Help! Help!" met her ears. It sounded as if it was coming from the direction of the upstairs bathroom.

Alex snapped her fingers. "Of course!" she said.

"What's the matter?" Melissa asked.

"Oh, nothing much. Rudy's stuck in the shower again," Alex answered quickly. "I'll be right back."

Running to the bathroom door, Alex shouted, "Rudy! I'm coming in!" She banged open the door.

"It's too hot! I can't turn it off!" Rudy wailed from behind the shower curtain.

"I'll get it!" Alex shouted to her little brother. She threw him a towel. "Here, wrap up in this."

Rudy wrapped himself in the towel and stepped out of the shower. Alex wrestled with the shower faucet. Water sprayed her hair and face as she whirled the faucet first one direction and then another. It was hard to remember which direction was on and which was off.

Ever since her father had insisted on replacing the leaky shower faucet himself, the family had had problems. The faucet now turned toward "hot" for cold water and "cold" for hot water. Alex's younger brother, Rudy, had the most trouble of all. He always seemed to turn the faucet the wrong way and the water would get so hot that he could not get close enough to turn it off.

"There you go, Goblin," Alex said to her

brother when she had finally turned off the water.

"Thanks, Alex," Rudy mumbled.

"What happened? Where did you go?" Melissa asked as soon as Alex had returned to her bedroom.

"Oh, I had to turn the shower off for Rudy," Alex replied. She flopped down on her bed and smiled at Melissa. Melissa was a new girl at school. At her mother's suggestion, Alex had invited Melissa to spend the night.

"Would you like to play a game?" Alex asked Melissa. "We have lots of board games, or we could play something on the computer."

"No . . . let's sneak out of the house and walk down to the school," Melissa suggested.

Alex looked at Melissa in surprise. "What for?" she asked.

Melissa shrugged. "It's something to do," she replied.

Alex glanced out her window. It was

almost dark. "It's too late. My parents wouldn't want us to do that."

"Of course they wouldn't." Melissa rolled her eyes. "But that's what makes it fun. Besides, they would never know."

"No, we'd better not." Alex shook her head. Her parents had a way of discovering those kinds of things, and Alex did not want to spend the first weekend of fifth grade grounded.

"Okay," sighed Melissa. "Let's go downstairs and hang out with your sister and her friends."

Alex's older sister, Barbara, and a group of her friends were listening to music in the family room.

"Naw," Alex wrinkled her nose. "Barbara wouldn't like having us around."

"So what?" Melissa scowled. "It's your house, too, isn't it?"

"Yeah, but . . ." Alex began.

"Who cares what your sister wants!" Melissa went on.

Alex was getting annoyed with Melissa.

"I care!" she exclaimed. "My sister and I have an agreement. She doesn't bother me when my friends are over, and I don't bother her and her friends."

Melissa just gave Alex a sarcastic smile.

"Uh . . . " Alex was almost afraid to suggest anything else. "Would you want to play Ping-Pong in the basement?"

Melissa sighed in a very bored way.

"Okay!" Alex threw her hands up in the air. "We can just watch television."

"Let's play Ping-Pong," Melissa finally said. "At least then we can walk through the family room on our way to the basement."

Alex shook her head as she followed Melissa down the stairs and through the family room. This evening had not started out well at all.

"It was awful!" Alex told her best friend, Janie, the next day. "All Melissa wanted to do were things that would get me in trouble. And then she'd get mad

11

when I told her we couldn't do those things.

"What's the matter with her?" Janie exclaimed. "Why did she want to get you in trouble?"

"It was like she didn't care," Alex told her friend. "She kept bugging Barbara until Barbara got really mad and told Mom and Mom got mad at me!"

"Oh, no!" Janie cried.

"Oh, it's okay," said Alex. "I explained it all to Mom and Barbara later, and they aren't mad at me anymore."

"That's good," replied Janie.

"There is one good thing about all of this," Alex said with a grin. "Mom doesn't want me to ask Melissa to spend the night again!"

"It's too bad Melissa's in your class at school," Janie observed. Janie and Alex were in different classrooms this year.

"Oh, it's no big deal," Alex replied. "I can just ignore her."

But when Alex got to school on

Monday, she found that she was the one who was ignored. None of the girls in her classroom would speak to her. Whenever Alex tried to start a conversation with them, the girls would walk away. However, Alex noticed that Melissa had no trouble talking to the girls. In fact, she seemed to be the center of their attention.

By lunchtime, Alex was angry and very lonely. Standing by herself in the lunch line, she felt as if she were the only one in the world without a friend.

*If only Janie were here,* she thought to herself. Why was Janie's class always late for lunch?

"Hel-lo, Al-ex," a sudden voice sang in her ear. It was Melissa. She was carrying a lunch tray. Before Alex knew what was happening, Melissa sprinkled a few peas on Alex's toes. Alex tried to jump out of the way but only managed to squish the peas under her feet.

"A few gross peas for a gross person!" Melissa called over her shoulder. She ran to a table and sat down quickly. Sitting at the table were the girls from Alex's class. They giggled at Melissa's joke.

Alex faced straight ahead in line. She did not look right or left. She ignored the giggles all around her.

Upon getting her lunch tray, Alex carried it to an empty table at the very back of the cafeteria. She sat down facing the wall. She did not want to look at anyone.

Blinking back hot, angry tears, Alex began to choke down her food. Angry, confused thoughts raced through her mind. Why were the girls treating her this way? What had she done? Alex could not think of one single thing that she had done to make them mad at her.

"Alex!" Janie suddenly called out from behind Alex's chair. "What are you doing at this table? I almost couldn't find you!"

She sat down next to Alex. Julie and Lorraine, two other friends, sat across from Alex and Janie.

"I'm surprised you even want to sit at the same table as me!" Alex snapped at her friends.

"Huh? What do you mean?" they asked.

"No one in my whole class wants to sit with me or talk to me," Alex exploded, "except Melissa Howard. She threw peas at my feet and called me gross!"

Janie, Julie, and Lorraine exchanged surprised glances. They listened carefully as Alex told them how the girls in her class would not speak to her.

"That's strange," Janie commented. "I wonder why nobody would talk to you?"

Alex shrugged her shoulders. "I can't think of one single reason."

"Well, it sounds like Melissa Howard is behind it all," declared Janie.

"Yeah," Alex agreed, "but why would she be mean to me? All I did was ask her to spend the night with me. You don't usually get mad at someone for that!"

Janie did not have an answer. Neither did Julie or Lorraine.

"Don't worry, Alex," Julie patted her arm. "We'll figure the whole thing out."

"Yeah, Alex, everything will be okay," Lorraine smiled.

Alex smiled back at her friends. Even if everything else went wrong, she was grateful for her three good friends.

At the last hour of the school day, Alex and several others walked down the hall to the band room. The fifth graders were joining the Kingswood School band for the first time.

Alex was excited. In her right hand she carried a large music case that contained a beautiful, shiny, brass trumpet. She had waited a long time for just such a trumpet, picturing in her mind how it would look when she held it to her lips and blew the most powerful blast of musical notes. And the best part of all was that it was her very own trumpet. Alex had already taken three lessons at the music store. She felt confident in her trumpet-playing ability.

In the band room, Alex hurried to an empty chair between Janie and Lorraine. Julie sat on the other side of Janie.

Janie and Julie each held small music cases on their laps. They were going to play flutes in the band.

"I hope they have enough baritones," Lorraine whispered to Alex. Lorraine wanted to play one of the school's large brass horns called a baritone. Alex thought the baritone would be good for Lorraine. After all, the baritone was big, and so was Lorraine.

Mr. Sharp, the band teacher, brought the class to order. "I want everyone to divide into groups according to your instruments," he said. "I want the drums over there," Mr. Sharp waved his hand in one direction, "and the trumpets and baritones over there," he waved in a different direction, "and the flutes over there. . . ."

Alex was surprised to find that she was the only girl in the middle of a group of

boys. Not one other girl had a trumpet.

Feeling odd and a little outcast, Alex flopped down in a chair at the end of a row. Much to her disgust, Eddie Thompson sat down next to her. Eddie was the class clown and generally caused as much trouble as he could. Lately, he had begun to carry sunflower seeds in his back pocket, shooting them at various targets.

Doing her best to ignore Eddie, Alex opened her trumpet case and pulled out her instrument. She stood it up on the other side of her chair—as far away from Eddie as possible. Then Alex grabbed the mouthpiece and had just started to fit it on to her trumpet when someone called, "Help, Alex, help!"

Alex whirled around. Lorraine sat in the row of chairs behind her. She was slumped over a baritone that sat on the floor. One of her arms seemed to be stuck inside the huge instrument.

"Help, help, it's eating my arm!" Lorraine cried.

Alex leaped off her chair and ran to rescue Lorraine.

"Ha! Ha! Ha!" Lorraine laughed as soon as Alex reached her side. "I was only kidding!" Lorraine easily popped her arm out of the baritone.

"Very funny, Lorraine," Alex chuckled.

Just then, Mr. Sharp called for order in the band room. Alex scurried back to her chair. When she reached it, to her dismay, Eddie Thompson had picked up her trumpet and was fiddling with it.

"Give me my trumpet!" Alex cried and snatched the instrument away from Eddie.

"Okay, okay," Eddie held up his hands. "Don't have a major hissy fit. I was just looking at it."

Alex checked her trumpet over carefully. Everything looked okay. But she was still uneasy. Had Eddie done something to her trumpet?

"We are going to begin learning the notes to a simple song," Mr. Sharp was saying, "but first, can anyone here play the C scale?"

Alex quickly looked up. She had learned to play the C scale in her first music lesson. She raised her hand.

"Okay, Alex," Mr. Sharp nodded. "Show us how the C scale should be played."

Quickly clamping the mouthpiece to her trumpet, Alex stood up and held it to her lips. She paid no attention to the giggling beside her. Let the boys laugh! She'd show them how good a trumpet player she really was.

Taking a deep breath, Alex blew, "BLEEEEEAAAAAHHHHH!" The note immediately went sour. A rattle sounded deep inside the trumpet. Then, try as she might, Alex could get no air to pass through the trumpet. She blew until her face was purple, but no sound came out of the trumpet.

The boys in her section practically rolled off their chairs in laughter. Eddie Thompson laughed the loudest of them all.

"EDDIE THOMPSON!" Alex screamed at the top of her lungs. "WHAT DID YOU DO TO MY TRUMPET?"

And then, because the day had not gone well for Alex and because Eddie grinned at her in such an exasperating way, Alex gave in to her angry feelings. SMACK! She whacked Eddie on top of his head with her music book.

Stunned silence filled the band room.

# CHAPTER 2

# Ugly Gossip

"Owwwwwwwwww!" moaned Eddie Thompson. He rubbed the top of his head where Alex had hit him.

"Alex, would you and Eddie like to explain what is going on between the two of you?" asked Mr. Sharp. He folded his arms across his chest and tapped his foot.

"Eddie did something horrible to my trumpet and now it won't play," Alex told her teacher. She demonstrated her point by once again blowing on her trumpet's mouthpiece. No sound came out.

Mr. Sharp replaced Alex's mouthpiece with his own and tried to play her trumpet. He could not get it to play either. He held it up to his ear and gently shook it. A faint rattle could be heard.

"Did you put something inside this instrument?" Mr. Sharp asked Eddie.

"Uh, well, I guess so," Eddie smiled sheepishly at the teacher. The other boys laughed.

"This is not funny!" Mr. Sharp told the boys with a frown. "If you cannot treat musical instruments with respect, there is no room for you in the band." He glared at Eddie. "You may sit in the time-out chair for the rest of the period."

"But what about Alex?" Eddie complained as he shuffled his way to the chair.

"Hmmmpf!" snorted Mr. Sharp. "If you had messed with one of my instruments, I might have hit you with something harder than a softcover music book!"

The class laughed. Eddie sat down in the time-out chair.

Mr. Sharp showed Alex how to flush out her trumpet with water at the sink in the back of the classroom. She watched carefully as Mr. Sharp took off the mouthpiece and pulled the tuning slide out of its place. He then ran a stream of water through the trumpet.

Almost immediately, two tiny objects floated out of the end of the instrument. Alex picked them up.

"Sunflower seeds!" she cried in a disgusted voice.

Mr. Sharp made Eddie empty his pockets of sunflower seeds. Alex returned to her seat with her newly restored trumpet. If this was how band class began, she was almost afraid to think about the rest of the year.

"The girls won't talk to *me* either!" Janie complained as she hurried down the sidewalk toward Alex.

Janie had stopped after school to ask Melissa and the other girls why they were not speaking to Alex.

Alex had waited for Janie outside. She frowned at Janie's report. "Why won't they talk to you?"

"Melissa says that no one can talk to

me because I'm your best friend!" Janie replied, coming to stand beside Alex.

"But I still don't know why they aren't speaking to me!" Alex exclaimed in frustration.

"I know," Janie shrugged her shoulders, "and we can't find out until they decide to talk to one of us again."

Alex stomped her foot angrily. "THIS IS RIDICULOUS! I HAVE DONE NOTHING WRONG TO ANY OF THOSE GIRLS!" she shouted.

"Come on, Alex," Janie said. She began pulling Alex down the sidewalk. Other children stared at Alex, surprised at her angry outburst.

"NERDS! THEY'RE ALL NERDS!" Alex shouted one more time. She angrily stomped down the sidewalk.

On reaching home, Alex said good-bye to Janie and rushed inside. She wanted to talk to her mother. She found Mother in the backyard, the garden hose in her hand, standing by a very wet and

25

unhappy-looking black dog. Mother's clothes were splotched with paint.

"What are you doing?" Alex asked.

"I'm giving T-Bone a bath," Mother answered. "He's been a very bad dog today."

"What did he do?" Alex wanted to know.

"Well, I was doing some painting in the basement," Mother explained, "and T-Bone sat down in the pan of paint."

"Oh, no!" Alex began to giggle.

"That's not all," Mother told her. "When he sat down, the paint pan flipped in the air. The paint splattered everywhere, but most of it landed on T-Bone's back!"

"Oh, poor T-Bone!" Alex laughed. She grabbed the soapy brush and began to scrub T-Bone's paint-splattered tail. While she worked, she told Mother about her problems with Melissa Howard and the girls in her class.

"Do you mean that *none* of the girls would speak to you?" Mother raised her eyebrows in surprise.

"The only girls in the fifth grade that would speak to me were Janie, Julie, and Lorraine," Alex replied, a disgusted look on her face.

"That's the silliest thing I have ever heard," declared Mother.

"Yeah, and it looks like Melissa Howard started it all," said Alex.

"Hmmmm." Mother thought for a moment. "You and Melissa didn't get along too well when she spent the night with you, but I didn't think you did anything to make her want to turn all the girls against you."

"I didn't do anything bad to her," Alex said. "So now, for no reason at all, Melissa's made up some stupid story about me and all the girls believe it." Alex stamped her foot. "They look at me and giggle and whisper to each other." To her dismay, Alex felt the tears gather in the corners of her eyes.

"Oh, honey, I'm sorry," said Mother. She put a wet, soapy arm around Alex.

"It's just not fair," Alex sobbed into her mother's shoulder. "I have been friends with those girls a lot longer than Melissa Howard. Why would they listen to her?"

"Oh, because she's filled their ears with some kind of juicy gossip about you," Mother replied.

"Juicy gossip?" Alex frowned. "I thought gossip was only for old ladies."

Mother laughed. "Oh, no, Alex, anybody can gossip. All you need is one person who wants to spread ugly, nasty rumors about someone else."

"But why would anyone want to do that?" Alex persisted.

"Because some people think that it's fun to gossip," Mother answered.

"That's sick!" exclaimed Alex.

"Yes, gossip is very 'sick,' as you say, and hurts a lot of people," said Mother.

"But what ugly rumors would Melissa want to spread about me?" Alex wondered.

"Why don't you call her and ask her?" Mother suggested.

"You mean call her on the telephone?" Alex's eyes opened wide at the idea.

"Sure, why not give it a try?" asked Mother. "Maybe she'll talk to you on the telephone and you can find out just what is going on."

"Great idea!" Alex threw the soapy brush to her mother and began to run across the backyard.

"Alex!" Mother called after her. "Where are you going?"

"Over to Janie's house!" Alex called

back. "I'm gonna get Janie to help me call Melissa!"

Alex was in such a hurry that she leaped over the fence that separated her backyard from Janie's backyard.

"JANIE! JANIE, ARE YOU THERE?" Alex bellowed through the screen door at the back of Janie's house.

"Why, hello, Alex," said Mrs. Edwards, Janie's mother. She opened the door for Alex. "Janie's in the kitchen."

Alex thanked Mrs. Edwards and hurried to the kitchen. She found Janie perched on a stool at a counter, busily shoving handfuls of tiny objects into her mouth.

"Are those sunflower seeds?" Alex demanded with her hands on her hips.

"Alex!" Janie exclaimed. "Where'd you come from?"

"Never mind! Are those sunflower seeds?" Alex repeated.

"Yes," Janie sighed.

"Janie! How could you eat sunflower

seeds after all the trouble those things have caused me today?" asked Alex.

"Sorry!"

"Come on, we've got a job to do," Alex dragged Janie off of her stool. "You gotta help me call Melissa Howard."

"What?" Janie stared at Alex in surprise. "Why?"

"Because I need to try and stop all the gossip," Alex answered.

"Gossip?" Janie echoed.

"Yeah, gossip! That's what you call it when people talk about you behind your back," Alex explained. "And I gotta find out what Melissa is saying that makes everyone not want to talk to me."

"Okay, let's do it," Janie agreed. She got out the Kingswood Elementary School telephone directory and handed it to Alex.

Alex dialed Melissa Howard's number. "Hello, Melissa, this is Alex Brackenbury—"

"Click!" The phone went dead. Alex pushed the receiver button up and down. The dial tone suddenly buzzed in her ear.

"That's funny," Alex said to Janie. "We must have got a bad connection. I'll call again."

"Hello, Melissa," she said after dialing the number once more, "this is Alex."

"I'm not speaking to you," hissed the voice on the other end of the line. "Click!" The phone went dead again.

"Brussels sprouts! She hung up on me!" Alex exclaimed. She banged down the receiver and stomped around the kitchen.

"Here, let me try," said Janie. She dialed Melissa's number.

"Hello, Melissa, this is Janie Edwards," Janie said into the receiver. "I would like to know why you aren't speaking to Alex."

Janie was silent for a moment as she listened to Melissa. "But can't you just tell me why . . ." Janie began.

There was silence. Then, suddenly, Janie slammed down the receiver. She, too, stomped around the kitchen. "She said she can't tell me anything because she's not speaking to me either!"

"But how are we ever going to find out what gossip Melissa is spreading around?" Alex wailed.

Janie looked at her friend sadly. "I don't know," she admitted.

"I suppose Melissa is laughing at us right now!" Alex fumed.

"Yeah and I suppose she's telling all of her friends how she wouldn't speak to us even on the telephone," added Janie.

"They used to be *our* friends," Alex reminded Janie.

The girls sank down on two of the stools at the kitchen counter. Janie held her head in her hands. Alex drummed the countertop with her fingers.

"Hey!" Alex cried suddenly. "I almost forgot! Julie was going to try and walk home with Melissa today. Let's see if she learned anything."

"Good idea," Janie reached for the telephone. "I'll call her."

"I'll get on the other phone," Alex called and ran into the next room. She picked up the receiver just as Julie answered on the other end.

"Hello, Julie, this is Janie."

"And Alex," added Alex from her phone.

"Oh, hi . . ." said Julie in what Alex thought was a rather unfriendly voice.

Janie didn't seem to notice. She told Julie how she and Alex had called Melissa and how Melissa would not talk to either of them.

"So we were wondering, were you able to find out anything from Melissa?" Janie asked Julie.

"Uh . . ." Julie hesitated. "Can I call you back later? I can't talk right now. My mom needs me."

"Oh, sure," Janie replied.

"Did Julie sound funny to you?" Alex asked when she had returned to the kitchen.

"Maybe a little," Janie answered. "She must have been busy with something."

"Maybe she really didn't want to talk to

us," Alex said, worried. "Maybe *she* has decided not to speak to us either!"

"Don't be ridiculous! Julie's our friend. She's not like the other girls."

"I guess you're right." Alex tried to smile. "I'm getting too worried about everything."

"Right! Loosen up!" Janie laughed. "Everything will be all right." She passed a package toward Alex. "Here, have some sunflower seeds!"

"Okay," Alex giggled, dumping a bunch of the seeds into her hand. "I oughta learn how to shoot these seeds so I can defend myself against Eddie Thompson."

Janie grabbed a pack of straws and she and Alex spent the rest of the afternoon learning to shoot sunflower seeds.

# CHAPTER 3

A
Deadly
Fall

The next day at school was absolutely awful. Just as Alex suspected, the girls in her class knew that she and Janie had tried to call Melissa the night before.

Alex's ears burned and her face turned red as she heard her name spoken again and again by the circle of girls at the back of the classroom.

"So she called Melissa last night," said a sarcastic voice.

"How dare she?" cried another voice.

"Doesn't she know we're not speaking to her?" a third, more nasty-sounding voice asked as they all giggled.

Alex slumped down in her seat. She noticed that a few boys were listening to

36

what the girls were saying. If the boys found out that the girls were not speaking to her, Alex would be horribly teased.

Fortunately for Alex, Mrs. Hibbits, her teacher, called for silence. Everyone had to sit down and class began.

As the morning wore on, things did not improve for Alex. She tried not to notice the cruel stares from the girls. Every time anyone whispered or giggled, Alex was sure the joke was on her.

By the time lunch rolled around, Alex was extremely upset. She waited impatiently for Janie and Lorraine and Julie to join her at the lonely end of the last cafeteria table.

"I'm so glad you're here," she cried in relief as Janie and Lorraine sat down on either side of her. Alex looked around.

"Where's Julie?" Alex asked Lorraine.

"Uh . . ." Lorraine hesitated and looked helplessly at Janie.

"She's over there!" Janie said angrily and pointed at a crowded table.

"WHAT!" Alex shouted. "YOU MEAN SHE . . . YOU MEAN SHE'S JOINED THAT GROUP?" Alex jumped up and loudly banged both hands on the table.

"Calm down, Alex," Janie hissed. "It's not going to help to scream about it. You'll only get in trouble."

"But . . . but . . . "Alex slowly sat down again. "I told you Julie sounded funny on the phone yesterday!"

"Yeah," replied Janie. "I guess you were right about her. I didn't think Julie would do such a thing!"

"Neither did I," sighed Alex.

That afternoon, Alex and Janie trudged up the steep Juniper Street hill on their way home from school. Ahead of them walked Alex's younger brother, Rudy, and his best friend, Jason.

The girls were silent. Each was thinking her own thoughts. Suddenly, Rudy buzzed a giant, blue plastic airplane in front of Alex's face.

"Goblin!" Alex cried, using her special nickname for her brother. "Cut it out!"

"Grouchhead!" Rudy called, sticking his tongue out at Alex. He and Jason skipped up the street ahead of the girls.

Alex sighed and looked at Janie. "I guess I have been sort of a grouch lately. It's just that everything at school has been going wrong."

"I know," Janie sympathized.

"I wanted things to go right, especially at the beginning of fifth grade."

"Yeah," Janie nodded her head. "Fifth grade shouldn't be like this. It should be, well, sort of grown up."

As the girls talked, they continued walking up the hill. They were so busy speaking to one another that they did not notice Rudy high up in a tree until he and Jason hollered down at them.

Looking up, Alex gasped. Rudy was in a very dangerous position. He had climbed up a monstrous old tree that grew beside the sidewalk and had crawled

along a fat limb that stuck out over the sidewalk. Apparently he had stopped his climb, too afraid to move out farther onto the limb and too afraid to inch his way backwards to the trunk. He had wrapped himself around the fat old limb and was holding on tight.

"BRUSSELS SPROUTS, GOBLIN!" Alex cupped her hands around her mouth and yelled her loudest. "GET DOWN FROM THERE BEFORE YOU KILL YOURSELF!"

"I CAN'T GET DOWN!" Rudy wailed.

"I TOLD HIM NOT TO GO OUT ON THAT LIMB," Jason called down to Alex. Jason was perched much lower in the tree than Rudy.

"WELL, WHAT'D HE GO OUT THERE FOR ANYWAY?" Alex asked Jason.

"TO GET HIS BLUE BOMBER!" Jason pointed to a spot near Rudy.

Alex squinted. There, close to where Rudy clung for dear life, was the tail end of the blue plastic airplane.

"Oh, brussels sprouts!" Alex sighed. "I suppose I have to go up and get him."

"Be careful, Alex," Janie warned. Janie was afraid to climb trees and did not like to watch other people do it.

Alex, however, loved to climb trees and for quite a while had had her eye on this particular tree. Its owner, however, was Mrs. Rudford, who, like Janie, was very nervous about children climbing trees. She had repeatedly told the neighborhood children that they were not to climb the trees in her yard.

Alex grinned as she scooted up the trunk of the tree. If Mrs. Rudford caught her climbing the tree, she would just say that she was trying to rescue her brother.

Quickly passing Jason, Alex pulled herself up alongside Rudy's limb. She could see why her brother was afraid to move. The wind was blowing hard at the top of the tree. The branches swayed back and forth. Even with Rudy on it, the fat old limb moved up and down in the wind.

"Okay, Goblin, you're gonna have to move back toward the trunk," Alex said. She was as close as she could get to Rudy without actually climbing onto the limb herself.

"I can't!" Rudy cried.

"You have to! There's no other way," Alex told her brother. "Just scoot backwards, a little at a time."

Rudy hesitated for a few moments, then, at Alex's insistence, he began inching his way back to the tree trunk.

"You're doing great, Goblin. You only have a little ways to go."

Just as Rudy got to where Alex could almost grab his foot, Mrs. Rudford stepped out on her front porch. She immediately spotted Alex and Rudy high up in her tree. Mrs. Rudford threw her hands in the air and screamed at the top of her lungs, "AHHHHHIIIIIEEEEEE!"

The cry was so unexpected and so loud that it badly frightened the children. Alex felt her heart jump in terror and only just managed to grab hold of the trunk to keep herself from falling.

Rudy did not have anything to grab, and already being terribly frightened of falling, lost his balance and rolled off of the limb. With a screech, he fell to the ground far below!

Alex screamed as she watched her brother hit the ground hard and then lie very still. He lay in a crumpled position. One of his arms was bent funny with the elbow pointing straight up at Alex.

"Why doesn't he move?" Alex asked herself. "Why doesn't he cry?" She waited for Rudy's shout of pain, but it didn't come. Everything was deathly quiet.

Alex forced her legs and arms to climb down the tree's trunk. As she neared the ground, she could see that Rudy's eyes were closed.

"He's not even awake!" she told herself. His face looked as white as a sheet. Was he breathing? Was he still alive?

# CHAPTER 4

# Hospital Prayers

"CALL THE POLICE! CALL THE AMBULANCE! OH, CALL SOMEBODY!" Mrs. Rudford ran about the yard shouting at the top of her voice.

Another time, Alex might have laughed at Mrs. Rudford's behavior. But right now, Alex was too worried about Rudy to laugh at anything.

"Rudy! Rudy! Can you hear me?" Alex called to her brother.

Rudy made no response. His face was so white. He made no movement whatsoever. Alex fought the fear that steadily rose in her throat. She forced herself to think.

What should she do? She needed a

grown-up. Mrs. Rudford was no help. She needed her mother. Should she run up the street to get her? No, she couldn't leave Rudy. Besides, that would take too much time. Her brother was badly hurt and needed an ambulance right away. There was no one else to do it. *She* would have to call an ambulance.

"Janie!" Alex shouted to her friend. "Go get my mom! Quick!" She watched as her best friend started up the street as fast as she could go.

"Jason, stay here with Rudy!" Alex commanded the younger boy. She trotted toward Mrs. Rudford's front door.

"Where are you going?" Jason shouted.

"I'm gonna call an ambulance!" Alex called over her shoulder.

Alex rushed into the house. She found the telephone in the kitchen. Taking a deep breath, Alex dialed the emergency number, 911. She had never dialed 911 before. She was nervous and terribly frightened.

"911—EMERGENCY!" a deep voice boomed on the other end of the line.

"Uh, hello?" said Alex. "I have an emergency."

"What kind of emergency, honey?" Immediately the deep voice softened.

"My brother fell out of a tree and he's hurt bad," Alex answered.

"Hold on," the voice responded. "I am transferring you to the ambulance dispatcher."

Alex heard a click on the line and then a lady's voice said, "Fire and Ambulance! Where do you need us?"

"Oh!" Alex wailed. "I don't know the address! I mean, I'm at a neighbor's house. It's on Juniper Street."

"The address has flashed on my screen," the woman told her. "Do you need an ambulance?"

"Oh, yes, please hurry!" Alex shouted. "My brother needs help!"

"The ambulance is on its way," replied the woman in a soothing tone. "What happened to your brother?"

"He fell out of a tree. It's a really big tree and he's just lying on the ground sorta crumpled up and he won't move or say anything." Alex's voice shook and hot tears began to sting her eyes.

"Is your brother unconscious?" the woman asked.

"Yes," Alex sniffed. She burst into tears and could not answer any more questions for a moment.

"How old is your brother?" the woman asked gently.

"He's eight years old," Alex finally managed to answer.

"And how old are you?"

"I'm ten."

"Is there an adult with you?" the woman asked.

"No," Alex answered. She did not count Mrs. Rudford. "But my best friend went to get my mother."

"Good," replied the woman. "Here's what I want you to do. Go back outside and stay with your brother until the ambulance comes. Can you do that?"

"Yes," Alex replied. She hung up the phone and wiped her eyes on her shirtsleeve.

Stepping outside, Alex breathed a sigh of relief. Both her mother and her older sister, Barbara, were there. They were bent over Rudy.

"I'm so glad you're here!" Alex shouted as she ran to them.

Mother looked up at Alex. She wore an anxious look. "Did you call an ambulance?" she asked.

"Yes, it should be here right away," Alex replied.

"Thank you, honey," said Mother. She grabbed Alex's hand and Barbara's hand and the three of them knelt beside Rudy.

"Please, Lord God," Mother prayed out loud. "Place Your loving hand on Rudy. Heal his injuries and restore him to us. In the name of Jesus, we pray."

At that moment, the ambulance

arrived. Its lights whirled and flashed. Alex could not help but think how excited Rudy would have been to see an ambulance in his neighborhood. If only he could see it. If only he wasn't hurt.

Two young men leaped from the ambulance and ran into the yard carrying a stretcher. In a few moments, they had loaded Rudy onto the stretcher and lifted him into the back of the ambulance.

Alex waved good-bye to Janie and Jason as she climbed into the ambulance with her mother and Barbara to ride to the hospital with Rudy.

Mother never stopped praying the entire way to the hospital. Alex prayed too. Over and over she whispered, "Help Rudy, Lord Jesus, help Rudy!"

When they reached the hospital, they were met by several people in white uniforms. Rudy was whisked inside. Mother followed the stretcher into a room. Barbara went to call Father. Alex was left to sit alone in the waiting room.

It wasn't long before tears began to slide down Alex's face. Sure, Rudy could be a pest sometimes and an absolute brat at other times. But all and all, he was a pretty good little brother, and Alex wanted to keep him.

"Oh, Barbara!" Alex cried as soon as her sister returned. "What if Rudy doesn't make it?"

Barbara sat down on the sofa next to Alex and hugged her younger sister. "He will make it," Barbara whispered. "I'm sure he'll be all right."

"But what if he's bleeding inside or what if he hurt his head really bad or what if—" worried Alex.

Barbara grabbed Alex's shoulders and looked straight into her eyes. "We have to trust God that none of those things have happened to Rudy," Barbara said firmly. "We have to believe that God is taking care of him, okay?"

Alex nodded, "Okay."

Suddenly, a tall, dark-haired man

burst though the door. He rushed over to Barbara and Alex.

"Dad!" Alex cried in surprise. Her father, normally so jolly, wore such a worried expression on his face that she had hardly recognized him.

"I came as quickly as I could," gasped Father. "Where's your mother and Rudy?"

"In that room." Alex and Barbara pointed to a set of double doors across the hallway.

At that moment, a nurse came up to Father. "Are you Mr. Brackenbury?" she asked.

"Yes," he answered.

"Please come with me," the nurse said. Father gave Alex and Barbara a weak smile and turned to follow the nurse.

"Wait, Dad!" Alex cried and ran to him. Taking his hand in hers, she told him, "Don't worry. I know the Lord will take care of Rudy."

A smile flickered across her father's face. "Thank you, Firecracker," he said, using his special nickname for Alex. "I needed to hear that."

It wasn't too long after Father left that Mother appeared. She was smiling and had good news. "Your brother does have a broken arm," she reported, "but the doctors can find nothing else wrong with him."

"Hurray!" Alex cried.

"Well, that's an answer to our prayers," Barbara exclaimed.

"I think you're right." Mother smiled. "The doctors said it was a miracle that Rudy wasn't seriously injured from such a high fall."

"Yeah, that was a long drop," Alex agreed. "I'll never forget how he looked lying unconscious under that tree." Alex's voice suddenly cracked with emotion.

"When I first saw him, I was so scared that I almost got sick," Barbara admitted.

"I know," Mother whispered. Tears slid down their faces as they hugged one another tightly.

Before they could dry their eyes, Father joined them in the waiting room. He no longer looked worried. Instead, he wore a happy smile.

"Firecracker," he said to Alex, "I hear you called the ambulance. That was a very brave thing to do."

"Thanks, Dad," replied Alex. She wriggled into her father's arms.

"By the way, your brother wants to see you," Father said to Alex.

"Me? He wants to see me?" Alex asked.

"Yes, he said something about a Blue Bomber," Father chuckled.

"Oh, no!" Alex exclaimed. "If he thinks I'm gonna go back up that tree to get his dumb airplane, he's crazy!"

Her family laughed. They walked, arm in arm, down the hallway to the hospital room where Rudy was resting.

Alex stared at her brother. He looked awfully small lying on such a high hospital bed. His face was still pale, but not as white as before.

"Hi, Goblin," Alex said as she stepped up beside the bed.

"Alex!" Rudy's eyes lit up when he saw her. "You gotta go rescue my Blue Bomber outa the tree."

"No!" Mother put a stop to it. "No one in this family is climbing that tree again!"

"I'm afraid, Rudy," chuckled Father, "that your Blue Bomber has become a permanent addition to Mrs. Rudford's tree."

Everyone laughed. Rudy let them admire the cast on his arm. It completely covered his left arm, running all the way from just under his shoulder to his wrist.

Soon, Alex, Barbara, and Mother got ready to go home. Father was going to stay with Rudy for a while. Then later, Mother would return to the hospital to spend the night with Rudy. The doctors wanted to keep Rudy overnight to make sure that he was all right.

"Bye, Goblin, see you tomorrow," Alex waved to her brother.

It was dark outside. Alex followed her mother and sister through the parking lot to where Father had parked his car. She breathed the cool night air and sighed in relief. Everything had turned out well. Rudy would be all right.

"Thank You, Lord Jesus," Alex whispered, looking at the bright, starry sky. "Thank You for saving Rudy."

# CHAPTER 5

# A Bathroom Fight

"Alex! Be careful!" Janie gasped, catching the giant punch bowl a second before it sailed off the end of the table.

Alex, while pulling a box of cookies out from underneath the table, had tried to stand up too soon and bumped the table, sending the punch bowl flying. Only Janie's quick move had saved the girls from disaster.

"Brussels sprouts! I just know something horrible is going to happen before the night is over," Alex worried. "I wish Mrs. Hibbits had never picked us to serve the cookies and punch at Back to School Night."

57

"Now, Alex," Janie scolded. "It's supposed to be an honor to serve the refreshments at Back to School Night."

"Well, it's not gonna be much of an honor if the punch bowl crashes to the floor and breaks into a hundred million pieces." Alex scowled. "I've almost knocked it off the table twice!"

"Just be more careful when you fill the cookie tray," replied Janie. She poked Alex in the ribs and smiled sweetly at a family with two young children approaching the refreshment table.

The mother of the two children picked up a glass of punch. She handed it to the small boy.

"I don't like this punch!" the boy cried after taking a small sip.

"MINE!" his little sister shouted and knocked the cup from his hand. The glass of punch splattered to the floor and left a bright, red puddle on the shiny gymnasium floor.

"OH, NO!" Janie and Alex wailed. They

58

rushed to wipe up the mess, but they did not get it cleaned up before Mrs. Larson, the school principal, saw it.

"GET THAT PUNCH OFF THE GYM FLOOR!" Mrs. Larson demanded, hurrying over to them. Her voice rang through the gymnasium, grabbing the attention of everyone in the room. People suddenly stopped their conversations to stare at Alex, Janie, and the spilled punch.

With the principal's help, the girls got the punch cleaned off the floor, but it was still sticky to the touch.

"Alex, go get some wet paper towels from the bathroom," directed Mrs. Larson.

Hurrying as fast as she could through the crowded hallways, Alex burst through the door of the nearest girls' bathroom. What she saw made her wish she had picked another bathroom—any other bathroom.

Right in front of Alex stood Melissa Howard and her best friend, Crystal

Dixon! They stared at her with fierce, frowning faces.

Alex was so surprised that, for a few moments, she could not speak. She stared back at the two girls. Dimly, she became aware of the sound of running water. Peering around Melissa and Crystal, Alex saw that the sinks in the bathroom were clogged with paper towels and water was pouring over their sides and onto the floor. Melissa and Crystal were flooding the bathroom deliberately!

"TURN OFF THE WATER!" Alex shouted at Melissa.

"NO!" Melissa shouted back.

"MAKE US!" taunted Crystal.

As Alex tried to move to the sinks, Crystal and Melissa blocked her way. "YOU'RE MAKING A MESS!" Alex cried.

"So what?" answered Melissa.

Alex could see that talking was getting her nowhere fast. All of a sudden, she lunged forward, faked to the left, and moved to the right. It was a good soccer fake and she had used it many times on the field.

The fake completely fooled Melissa and Crystal. Before they could recover, Alex had reached one of the sinks and had turned off the water.

"LEAVE THE SINKS ALONE!" Melissa cried and called Alex a bad name. She rushed at Alex with her fists flying.

Alex took aim and swung her fist as hard as she could at Melissa's chin. POW! Melissa fell backwards onto the wet floor. Alex then turned toward Crystal. Crystal backed away. She grabbed Melissa and the two girls fled out the door.

Breathing deeply, Alex tried to control the anger that burned inside of her. Her arms and legs shook. She moved unsteadily from sink to sink, turning off all of the faucets.

Just as she shut the last faucet off, the door opened and in walked Mrs. Larson. "Alex, why is it taking you so long to get the paper . . ."

The last words died on the principal's lips as she stared in disbelief at the water disaster.

"WHAT IS GOING ON HERE?" she demanded. The frown on her face looked absolutely frightening.

"I didn't do it," Alex squeaked as she stood on her wobbly legs and endured the principal's angry stare. Alex was so upset that her stomach seemed to flip-flop. She sank down on the floor, not caring that it was covered with water.

"Oh, Alex, I am sorry," Mrs. Larson said, squatting down beside her. "I didn't mean to accuse you. Besides," she said rubbing her chin in an attitude of deep thought, "now that I think about it, I know who did it."

"You do?" Alex asked surprised.

"I believe so," answered the principal. "I saw Melissa Howard and Crystal Dixon just before I walked in here. Both girls looked terribly upset, and Melissa's dress was wet. I wondered what they were up to. They are the ones who caused this mess, aren't they?"

Alex nodded and sighed in relief. It was good that Mrs. Larson knew the truth, and the best part about it was that Alex had not had to tell on Melissa and Crystal.

"Come on, Alex." Mrs. Larson helped Alex to stand. "We need to get you out of here. Oh! Look at the back of your dress. It's sopping wet."

"Oh, that's okay," Alex replied. "It's just

a dumb old dress."

Mrs. Larson chuckled. "It's nice to see you in a dress for a change, Alex."

Alex wrinkled her nose in disgust. She did not like wearing dresses. They were uncomfortable, and she couldn't pitch a softball or dribble a soccer ball in a dress!

When Alex returned to the gym, she found her mother helping Janie serve the punch and cookies.

"What happened to your dress?" Mother asked as soon as she saw Alex.

Alex told Mother and Janie all that had happened. Mother put her arms around Alex. "I'm sorry," she said. "I'll go get your father. We need to get you home and out of that wet dress."

"Sorry I have to leave," Alex apologized to Janie.

"Oh, that's okay," Janie replied. "You know, Alex, you were right about one thing."

"What's that?" Alex asked.

"You were right when you said

something horrible was going to happen tonight," Janie reminded her.

"Oh, yeah," Alex agreed, "I guess it happened."

When Alex got home, she went immediately to her room and changed clothes. After a few minutes, Mother knocked on her door.

"Come in," Alex called.

"I thought you might like some company," Mother said, opening the door. "You just went through a pretty rough time tonight."

"You can say that again," replied Alex. She sat on her bed with her chin in her hands. "I just don't understand why all this bad stuff has to happen to me!" she complained. "I don't know why Melissa was so mad at me in the first place and why none of the other girls would talk to me. It's so unfair!"

"Gossip is a terrible thing," said Mother. She slipped her arm around

Alex's shoulders. "I think the hurts that people give to each other with their tongues do far more damage than the hurts they give each other with their fists."

"So do I," Alex nodded. "You kind of forget about how much it hurts when somebody hits you. But, when somebody says something mean about you, the words stay in your memory for always. I don't think you ever really forget them."

"You're so right," Mother agreed. "Did you know the Bible says that we corrupt our whole bodies when we say something bad?"

"We do?" Alex asked, surprised.

"The apostle James said that just as a small bit in a horse's mouth can direct such a large animal or as a small rudder can turn a big ship, so our small tongues can turn our bodies to good or to evil depending on what we say."

"Wow!" Alex exclaimed. "I knew that if I said something mean about some- one else it would hurt them, but I didn't know that it would hurt me, too."

"Oh, yes," Mother nodded. "Gossip is like poison. You need only a small amount to do serious harm."

"Brussels sprouts! Melissa Howard must be full of poison!" Alex exclaimed.

"I'm afraid Melissa and the other girls don't realize how much they are hurting themselves by spreading gossip," said Mother sadly.

"But once gossip gets started, how do you stop it?" Alex wanted to know.

"Well, the best way to stop gossip is to refuse to listen to it," replied Mother. "If people wouldn't listen to gossip, then there would be no way to pass it on."

"The girls in my class have already listened to gossip about me," said Alex. "Even my good friend Julie."

"Do you know what they are saying about you?" Mother asked.

"No!" Alex crossed her arms over her chest and frowned. "No one will speak to me, so I can't find out what they're saying."

"Oh, dear," sighed Mother. "That is a bad situation. I don't see how you can prove that the gossip is wrong unless you know what it is."

"Right, and after tonight, Melissa will be so mad at me that she'll probably spread even more gossip," worried Alex. "Melissa and Crystal will think that I spoiled their fun and that it was my fault Mrs. Larson found out who did it. And then I'm in big trouble! I might as well change schools or something."

"Oh, Alex," Mother cried. "It won't be that bad, will it?"

"No," said Alex grimly. "It will be worse!"

# CHAPTER 6

# Adventure with T-Bone

When Alex got to school the next day, she found a note inside her desk. The note said, "If you tell on us, you are dead meat!" Small drops of blood dripped from each letter.

The note had to be from Melissa and Crystal. Throwing it back in her desk, Alex stared straight ahead. She pretended not to notice the mean looks from Melissa and Crystal. Let them think what they wanted. She had not been a tattletale. Mrs. Larson had figured out by herself who had messed up the bathroom.

Alex tried to concentrate on Mrs. Hibbits's geography lesson. She could feel the girls' eyes staring at her back.

Mrs. Hibbits was just winding up her

lesson when a commanding figure stepped into the classroom. It was Mrs. Larson and she was not smiling. She whispered something to Mrs. Hibbits.

"Melissa Howard and Crystal Dixon," Mrs. Hibbits called. "You are to go with Mrs. Larson at once."

Melissa shot an angry look at Alex before following the principal out of the door. When Crystal got up, she glared at Alex all the way out of the classroom.

Alex felt her cheeks grow hot. She knew everyone in the classroom was staring at her.

Quickly, Alex bent over her geography book. Hot tears sprang to her eyes. It wasn't fair! She had done nothing wrong, and yet, *she* was getting mean looks.

By morning recess, Melissa and Crystal still had not returned to class. They had not returned by lunchtime. After lunch, during afternoon recess, Alex, Janie, and Lorraine sat on the swings and discussed the matter.

"Why would Mrs. Larson keep Melissa and Crystal in her office this long?" Alex worried.

"Alex! Stop worrying!" Janie ordered. "You did not do anything wrong. It was Melissa and Crystal who flooded the bathroom."

"That's easy for you to say," Alex retorted. "You didn't get the note about being 'DEAD MEAT'!"

"I have a feeling we might all be dead meat real soon," Lorraine suddenly said. "LOOK!" She pointed at a large group of girls marching across the playground and heading straight for Alex and her friends.

"OH, NO!" Janie shouted.

"RUN!" cried Lorraine.

"NO!" Alex held up her hand. "We will not run away! Like Janie says, we have done nothing wrong."

The three girls sat on the swings and nervously waited for the group of girls to reach them. It took all of Alex's willpower to force herself to sit quietly and wait

71

when she really wanted to get up and run.

The girls soon surrounded Alex, Janie, and Lorraine. They all looked angry.

"What happened to Melissa and Crystal?" one of the girls demanded.

"How should I know?" Alex shrugged.

"We think you know," another girl said gruffly. "They gave you some awful looks before they left the room."

"Yeah, maybe it was your fault that they were getting in trouble," added another girl.

"It was not my fault!" Alex shouted. "I did nothing to them."

"That's right!" hollered Janie, who could no longer keep still. "Melissa and Crystal got themselves in trouble!"

"Oh, yeah?" one girl sneered. "And how did they do that?"

Janie and Alex looked at each other. "I guess we might as well tell you," Alex finally said. "Nobody said we shouldn't."

Alex told the girls how she had caught Melissa and Crystal stopping up the sinks and how Mrs. Larson had guessed who had done it.

When Alex finished, most of the girls were frowning. "Why would anyone want to flood a bathroom?" one of them asked.

"No wonder Mrs. Larson was so mad," said someone else.

The group of girls left the swing area, chatting among themselves. Alex, Janie, and Lorraine were alone once again.

"Brussels sprouts!" Alex exclaimed. "I'm glad that's over."

"Me, too," Lorraine agreed. "But did you notice that the girls sounded disgusted at what Melissa and Crystal did?"

"Maybe they'll decide that Melissa is not such a great person after all," Janie added.

"Maybe." Alex's face brightened. "But one good thing has happened for sure. The girls actually spoke to me for the first time all week!"

Janie and Lorraine laughed.

"Did you hear the news?" Janie called to Alex and Lorraine as she ran to meet them after school.

"You mean the news about Melissa and Crystal?" Alex asked.

"Yeah, they are suspended for two days!" Janie exclaimed.

"I know," Alex replied. "That's what everybody's talking about."

"Well, don't you think that's great?" Janie asked. "Now you don't have to see Melissa for two whole days, and maybe you can get to be friends again with the other girls before she comes back."

"Right!" agreed Lorraine. "Then Melissa couldn't do anything about it."

"Sounds good to me!" Alex laughed, leading the way down the sidewalk, across the street, and up the Juniper Street hill. "Why do you think Melissa is so mean?" Alex asked.

"Some kids are mean because their parents are mean to them," Janie replied.

"Or, because they are left alone a lot,"

added Lorraine. She was spending the afternoon with Alex and Janie.

"I wonder where Melissa lives," said Alex.

"We could look up her address in the school directory," Janie suggested.

"Let's do it!" agreed Alex. The girls ran the rest of the way to Alex's house.

Bursting through the front door, Alex led the way to the kitchen. "Hi, Mom!" she called. "We're going to look up Melissa's address in the school directory."

"Whatever for?" Mother asked.

"Oh, we were just wondering where she lives," Alex answered.

Mother shook her head as she set a plate of cookies out on the table.

"Here's her address," Alex announced. She picked up a cookie. "It's 6814 Locust," she said between bites.

"Locust?" Janie repeated. "I wonder where that is?"

"It's gotta be close," said Lorraine. "It's a street named after a tree, and all the streets in this neighborhood are named after trees."

"Locust is the name of a tree?" asked Janie. "I thought it was a bug."

Alex and Lorraine laughed. "It's also the name of a tree," they told Janie.

"The reason all the streets around here are named after trees is because this area is called Kingswood," explained Alex. "My dad says that he likes to think that we are living in the 'King's woods.' And since Jesus is the King of our lives, it means we're living in Jesus' woods!"

"That's pretty neat," Lorraine exclaimed. "I never would have thought of that!"

Just then, T-Bone, the family's black Labrador, came into the kitchen, trying to crowd up to the table with the girls.

"Oh, this dog!" Mother exclaimed. "He has been following me around all day. I think he's bored!"

"We'll entertain him, Mom," Alex volunteered. "Come on, T-Bone, we'll take you for a walk."

The big dog barked joyously and bounded to the front door. Alex ran to get his leash and snapped it onto his collar. T-Bone pulled Alex out of the door and led the girls down Juniper Street hill at a fast pace.

"Slow down, T-Bone!" Alex hollered. "You're gonna jerk my arm off!"

"Something tells me T-Bone is glad to get out of the house," laughed Janie.

"You can say that again!" Alex agreed. "Whoa, T-Bone!"

The walkers briskly moved on down the hill and around the curve to Maple Street. "There's creepy Julie's house," hissed Janie.

"I still can't believe she deserted us to be Melissa's friend," Lorraine said angrily.

Alex said nothing. She had been deeply hurt by Julie's actions. She did not want to talk about it.

They moved on up Maple Street, passing Walnut, Ash, and Elm Streets. They came to a busy intersection. On the other side of the intersection was a park.

"Oh, let's take T-Bone to the park!" Janie cried.

"Okay," Alex agreed. "He would like that."

Alex pushed the button on the traffic light pole to stop the busy traffic. Automobiles screeched to a halt. The girls and T-Bone began to cross the street. All of a sudden T-Bone saw something that made him very excited.

On the other side of the street was a

female black Labrador. She looked straight at T-Bone and wagged her tail. Then she began to run across the street. As she streaked past T-Bone, she glanced over her shoulder and looked to see if T-Bone would follow her.

T-Bone did just that. Before Alex knew what was happening, the big dog jerked the leash from her hands and took off after the female dog.

"STOP!" Alex hollered. "T-BONE! COME BACK HERE!"

Just then, the traffic light changed to green. Cars began to move forward. Janie grabbed Alex and pulled her, along with Lorraine, to safety on the other side of the street. Alex gasped and watched in horror as T-Bone turned suddenly to come back across the street in front of the cars.

"T-BONE!" she screamed. "GO BACK! YOU'LL BE KILLED!"

# CHAPTER 7

# Dog in the Mall

Tires squealed and cars screeched to a stop, barely missing T-Bone and the female Labrador. The dogs, however, did not seem concerned. They scampered on across the street, past Alex, and into the park beyond.

"T-BONE!" Alex shouted, stamping her feet. "YOU COME HERE!" But the big dog continued to run with his new friend.

Alex, Janie, and Lorraine chased the dogs as fast as they could. The dogs led them out the other side of the park and into an unfamiliar neighborhood.

Alex felt her legs tire as she ran after T-Bone up one street and down another. Finally, the dogs halted in front of a small, white house. The female dog lay down on the front porch. T-Bone stood and gazed at her, as if he did not know what to do. Alex stumbled into the yard and grabbed T-Bone's leash.

"T-BONE, YOU BIG MUTT!" she gasped and sank down beside him for a rest. The big dog gave her face a lick.

"ACK!" Alex cried. "Keep your old slobbery kisses to yourself. I'm mad at you!" She stood up. "Come on, we'd better get out of this yard." Alex dragged T-Bone over to the sidewalk and down the street toward Janie and Lorraine, who had dropped far behind in the chase.

Janie had a few things to say to T-Bone. She was telling him how some people eat "dog stew" when she was suddenly interrupted.

"Hey, look!" Lorraine exclaimed, pointing to the street sign.

It took Alex and Janie awhile to figure out why Lorraine was so excited. The street sign said, "Locust Drive."

"Locust!" Alex cried. "That's Melissa's street."

Janie wasn't so sure. "The directory said 'Locust.' It didn't say 'Locust Drive,' " she pointed out.

"That's because there's not enough room in the directory to print the whole address," Alex told Janie.

"Well, then maybe 'Locust' means 'Locust Street' instead of 'Locust Drive,' " argued Janie.

"Let's look and see if Melissa's house is on this street," Alex suggested. "If it is, then we'll know she lives on Locust Drive."

"Okay," Janie agreed.

"Uh, does anybody remember the house number?" asked Lorraine.

"Oh, sure," Alex replied. "It was 6814 or 6815 or something like that."

"I think it was 6816," said Janie.

"Well, whatever." Alex led the way down Locust Drive. "Let's look for those numbers and then narrow it down."

"What do you mean 'narrow it down'?" Janie asked with a frown.

"We can look for a name on the mailbox or something," answered Alex.

The girls and T-Bone walked all the way to the end of the block. They stopped at a stoplight marking another busy intersection.

"Now what do we do?" Janie complained. "The street numbers on Locust Drive end with 6679. We didn't even come to the 6800s."

"I bet Locust continues on the other side of this intersection," Alex guessed, gazing across the busy street. She shaded her eyes with her hand. "Can anybody read the street sign over there?"

"I think it starts with an 'L,' " Lorraine answered.

"Maybe we shouldn't go any farther," Janie said. "We've walked a long ways. Does anybody have a watch? My mom wants me home by five."

Nobody had a watch.

"It can't be five yet," Alex insisted. "Let's cross the street and see if Locust Drive is on the other side. If it's not, we'll turn around and go back home."

"And what if it is?" Janie asked.

"If it is Locust Drive," Alex continued, "we'll find Melissa's house real fast and then turn around and go home."

When the traffic light turned green, the girls and T-Bone scampered across the busy street. On the other side, Alex was pleased to find that Locust Drive did indeed continue.

"See! What did I tell you?" Alex shouted joyfully. She began to skip down the street with T-Bone trotting beside her. Janie and Lorraine followed close behind.

Suddenly, Locust Drive bent sharply to the left. A street sign marked the bend, showing that the street was now called Sycamore Lane.

"Sycamore Lane!" Alex exclaimed. "What happened to Locust?"

"It disappeared!" Lorraine shouted.

"That's ridiculous." Janie stamped her foot.

"It's a short block," Alex observed. "I can see another street sign up the way. Let's go see if it turns back into Locust Drive."

The girls charged up the block. Sure enough, at the next bend in the road, the street sign again read, "Locust Drive."

"Come on!" Alex laughed. "Locust Drive goes up that hill. Last one up is a rotten egg!" She and T-Bone sprinted forward. Soon they were panting. The street was not very long, but it was very steep. Reaching the top of the hill, Alex came to an abrupt stop.

"Brussels sprouts!" she gasped. "Hey! Look at this!"she called.

"Guess I'm the rotten egg," Janie grumbled as she reached Alex a step or two behind Lorraine.

"WOW!" she cried, and so did Lorraine, when they saw what was on the other side of the hill.

Locust Drive plunged straight down and at its bottom sprawled the giant Kingswood Shopping Mall.

"Can you believe we just reached the mall?" Alex asked.

"We must be a long ways from home," Lorraine commented.

Janie and Alex stared at Lorraine.

"Uh, I think you're right, Lorraine," Alex slowly said. She turned around and looked behind her. "I'm not sure of the way back home."

"Neither am I," Janie said. "We've twisted and turned so much that I'm all mixed up on my directions."

"It's getting dark," Lorraine pointed out. "Look! The streetlights are turning on."

"It must be after five," Janie sighed. "I'm gonna be in big trouble."

"Sorry, Janie," Alex patted her best friend's shoulder.

"What do we do now?" Lorraine asked.

"Let me think." Alex held up her hand.

"I know!" she said after a moment's thought. "We'll go down to the mall, find a telephone, and call my mom. Then, she can pick us up."

"Great idea!" Janie and Lorraine agreed. The girls and T-Bone hurried down the hill. They ran through the parking lot to one of the mall entrances.

"See, there's the telephones," Alex announced as they stared through the glass double doors. "I'll just run inside and call my mom. You stay here with T-Bone." She gave Janie the dog's leash and hurried inside. A moment later, she returned with a sheepish look on her face.

"Uh, anybody got a quarter?" she asked.

"Oh, brother," Janie rolled her eyes skyward. She and Lorraine fished through their pockets. They both came up empty-handed.

"Now what do we do?" Janie wailed.

"Wait a minute, " Alex replied, trying to act calm. "Don't panic. We'll think of something."

The three girls sat down on the sidewalk outside the double doors to think. T-Bone patiently sat beside them.

"I've got it!" Lorraine suddenly cried.

Alex and Janie looked at her in surprise. Lorraine hardly ever came up with ideas.

"You know that little booth in the middle of the mall where a lady sits and helps you if you have any questions?"

"The Information Booth!" Alex and Janie cried together.

"Great idea, Lorraine!" Alex clapped her friend's back. "We can go there for help." She was so relieved that she swung Lorraine around in circles. This made T-Bone so excited that he barked and jumped until he became completely tangled in his leash.

"Who's going to stay outside with T-Bone?" Janie wondered.

Alex stared at Janie hopefully.

"Don't look at me. What if he decided to run away again? I couldn't catch him."

Alex turned to Lorraine.

"Oh, no," Lorraine cried. "I'm kind of scared of dogs."

"Okay," Alex sighed. "I'll stay outside with T-Bone. You two go to the Information Booth and call my mom."

"What? I can't call your mom and tell her to come and get us at the shopping mall," cried Janie. "She might yell at me."

"Then call your mom," said Alex.

"That's worse!" Janie retorted. "I *know* my mom would yell at me!"

"How about you, Lorraine? Would you call my mom?" Alex asked without much hope. Lorraine was much more timid than Janie.

Lorraine shook her head and looked down at the ground.

"Can't we all go in?" Janie pleaded. "Maybe no one would notice T-Bone."

Alex glanced at the giant black dog sitting beside her and laughed. "Are you kidding?" she asked Janie.

"It's too bad we don't have a stroller to

put T-Bone in," Lorraine giggled. "We could disguise him as a baby."

"Disguise him?" Alex repeated. A smile began to spread across her face. She took off her sweatshirt and slipped it over the dog's head. With quite a struggle, she managed to get his long legs through the armholes. She then tied the hood in place. T-Bone did not like the hood at all and shook his head from side to side.

"You might as well get used to the hood and stop shaking your head," Alex told the dog. She opened the doors to the mall. "Come on." She grinned as she led T-Bone inside.

Janie and Lorraine could not stop giggling. They followed Alex and T-Bone into the stream of people shopping in the mall.

"Hurry up," Alex called to them. "You need to walk on either side of T-Bone to help hide him."

"Oh, Alex!" Janie covered her face with her hands. "This is so embarrassing!"

Lorraine was embarrassed, too. She would not even look at the people who stopped and pointed at T-Bone.

Alex ignored the laughter and the stares of the people around them. She and the dog moved straight ahead as if it were the most natural thing in the world to bring a dog to a shopping mall.

"Uh oh, brussels sprouts!" Alex suddenly cried. "I see a policeman!"

"Where?" Janie and Lorraine asked together.

"Straight ahead," Alex replied, "and he's coming this way."

"What do we do?" her friends cried.

"Let's walk on the other side of this crowd of people," Alex directed. "Maybe the policeman won't see T-Bone."

The girls and the dog moved to the far side of a group of older women who were walking past a line of shops. Alex and T-Bone slowed their pace. So did Janie and Lorraine. T-Bone was well hidden behind large shopping bags and purses.

Everything might have gone well except that, at that moment, the group of shoppers was passing by a meat and cheese shop. The shop owner was just setting up a table full of sausage samples. The sausages had been freshly grilled and cut into bite-sized pieces for people to taste. There was one thing, however, that the owner of the shop had not taken into consideration. He had not counted on a dog passing by his display, and certainly not as big a dog as T-Bone.

T-Bone's nose was on the same level as the table of sausages. He could not help but smell the wonderful aroma of freshly cooked sausage. As soon as he reached the table, the dog could not resist snatching an entire plate of sausages. He wolfed it down before anyone could even think to try and stop him.

"HEY!" shouted the shop owner in surprise. "A DOG ATE MY SAUSAGES!"

For a quick moment, Alex stared into the angry eyes of the shop owner. She did not know what to say or do. But T-Bone, frightened by the shouts of the shop owner, did know what to do. Jerking his leash out of Alex's hands, the dog bounded away, a half-eaten sausage hanging from his mouth.

"SOMEBODY STOP THAT DOG!" the owner yelled.

In his haste, T-Bone bumped squarely into the group of older women. Purses and packages flew every which way.

"HELP! HELP!" the women cried.

"T-BONE!" Alex yelled. "COME BACK HERE!" Stumbling over purses and bags, Alex ran up the mall in pursuit of the big dog.

Suddenly the loud shriek of a police whistle sounded in Alex's ears.

"STOP!" hollered the policeman. "STOP AT ONCE!"

But Alex could not stop—at least not until she had caught T-Bone. She was afraid the dog might get hurt or someone might steal him or he might dash outside and be lost forever!

"STOP! STOP!" the policeman continued to shout. Alex cringed. She was in a lot of trouble now. Would she be arrested and put in jail?

# CHAPTER 8

# T-Bone's Disaster

Alex dodged shoppers, strollers, and small children as she sped down the center of the mall after T-Bone. Tripping over a shopping bag, Alex crashed into one woman, causing her to drop all of her packages.

"I'm sorry!" Alex called over her shoulder. She continued to chase after the dog.

T-Bone himself was causing quite an uproar. People quickly moved out of his way. Adults and children alike laughed and pointed at the big dog galloping through the shopping mall, dressed in Alex's sweatshirt.

"T-BONE! COME BACK!" Alex shouted again. She glanced back. The policeman was gaining on her.

Picking up speed, Alex nearly caught T-Bone who had slowed his pace to sniff the wonderful smells from a pizza stand.

"Now I've got you!" Alex gasped. She reached out to grab the dog's collar, but T-Bone did not want to be caught yet.

"COME BACK!" Alex wailed as the big dog bounded away. Suddenly, a giant hand gripped her shoulder. Looking up, Alex stared into the stern eyes of the policeman.

"Please, let me go," Alex squeaked. "I need to get my dog."

"We will get your dog in a minute," the policeman coolly replied. "First, I would like to know who you are."

"Uh, my name is Alex Brackenbury."

"Well, Alex Brackenbury," the policeman repeated, "don't you know that it's against the law to bring a dog into a shopping mall?"

Alex gulped, but before she could answer, a loud scream followed by a thunderous crash sounded from the pottery shop next door.

Alex and the policeman ran to see what was the matter. Looking in the door of the shop, Alex gasped in alarm. A giant display of dishes had somehow fallen, making a mountain of rubble.

Several customers stood pressed against the walls of the shop to avoid being hit by flying pieces of pottery. A salesclerk hid behind a counter.

Upon seeing Alex and the policeman, the clerk slowly stood up. The customers stepped away from the walls.

A sudden whimpering noise sounded in the rear of the store. A dining-room table stood at the back of the shop. The table was covered with a white lace tablecloth and was set with beautiful blue- and gold-tone pottery dishes. But the sight that made Alex's heart sink to the bottom of her toes was the dog's head peeking around the corner of the table.

"T-Bone," Alex sighed in frustration. "Come here!"

Immediately, Alex realized that it had been the wrong thing to say. Terribly frightened, T-Bone rushed to Alex's side. In doing so, his big, black tail caught on the lace tablecloth and pulled it along behind him. The tablecloth and dishes fell to the floor! CRASH! BAM!

Alex closed her eyes and held her hands over her ears. T-Bone whimpered at her side.

"GET THAT DOG OUT OF HERE!" the salesclerk screamed.

"You go sit over there on that bench," the policeman directed Alex, pointing to a bench not far from the pottery shop. "And take your dog with you!"

The policeman entered the shop to try and help the salesclerk. Alex and T-Bone shuffled to the bench and collapsed on it. T-Bone, knowing he had done something wrong, laid his head on Alex's lap.

"Alex!" someone whispered right behind her.

Alex turned her head. Janie and

Lorraine stood behind the bench.

"Did you see what T-Bone did?" Alex asked her friends.

"Yeah, we heard the crash," Janie replied, shaking her head.

"What's the policeman going to do?" asked Lorraine.

"I don't know, but I think we're in big trouble!" Alex stroked T-Bone's head. The dog looked mournfully up at her.

It wasn't long before custodians and security guards arrived at the pottery shop. The policeman approached the bench where Alex, T-Bone, Janie, and Lorraine sat.

"Are these your friends?" he asked Alex, pointing to Janie and Lorraine.

Alex nodded.

"Are any of your parents here in the mall?" he asked.

They shook their heads.

"Then all of you better come with me."

The girls and T-Bone followed the policeman into an office-lined hallway that ran off of the main section of the mall. The policeman led them into one of the offices.

Seating himself behind a desk, the policeman motioned the girls to sit on chairs. He leaned forward and stared at them.

"Did you girls know that it is against city law to bring an animal into a shopping mall?" the policeman asked.

No one answered right away. Alex looked at Janie and Lorraine. They had scrunched as far down in their chairs as possible and both stared at the floor. Alex knew it was up to her to answer the policeman's question.

"Uh, I knew we weren't *supposed* to bring a dog into the mall," Alex admitted to the policeman, "but I didn't know it was against the law."

"Why did you bring your dog into the mall?" the policeman asked.

"We were looking for the Information Booth," Alex answered. "We needed to call my mom but we didn't have a quarter for the pay phones." Alex went on to tell the policeman how they had been lost and had decided to call Alex's mom from the shopping mall.

"I'm awfully sorry," Alex ended. "I didn't mean for T-Bone to eat all those sausages or break all those dishes."

Turning to her dog, Alex scolded, "T-Bone! If you'd keep your nose out of things, you wouldn't get into so much trouble!"

A chuckle escaped the lips of the policeman. Becoming serious again, he said, "Even though you did not mean for it to happen, your dog has done considerable damage to someone else's property. You also have broken a city ordinance by letting the dog into the mall. I'm afraid I will have to call all of your parents."

Janie and Lorraine gasped in alarm. Alex was not surprised. She had already figured that her parents would be called because of the damage T-Bone had done.

The girls gave the policeman their telephone numbers and waited nervously while he called their parents. Within minutes, the three sets of parents arrived at the mall.

"Oh, Alex, we were so worried about you!" cried Mother as soon as she saw Alex. "Why didn't you call home?"

"That's why we came into the mall in the first place," Alex tried to explain. "We were going to call you. . . ."

"Because we got lost and couldn't find

our way back home," Janie interrupted.

"Because T-Bone started chasing another dog and led us far away from our neighborhood," Lorraine added.

"And because *someone* just had to follow Locust Drive to find Melissa's house," said Janie, giving Alex an exasperated look.

"You wanted to find her house, too!" Alex snapped at Janie.

"GIRLS! GIRLS!" the policeman held up his hands. "Let's tell the story one at a time. Alex, you go first."

A few chuckles came from the grown-ups when they heard how T-Bone had snatched the sausages. But when Lorraine finished the story by telling how T-Bone had smashed the dishes in the pottery shop, no one laughed. The only noise was a loud groan from Alex's father. "I guess we had better go look at the damage," he said.

The grown-ups walked down the mall to the pottery shop. Alex and T-Bone stayed behind with Janie and Lorraine. Alex had no desire to see the salesclerk again—ever!

When her parents returned, all that Alex's father said was, "Most of it should be covered by insurance."

After promising the policeman that they would never again bring a dog into the shopping mall, the girls left with their parents. Alex waved good-bye to Janie and Lorraine as she climbed into the back-seat of her family's car.

Alex's father did not start the car right away. Instead, he turned around and looked at Alex as she sat in the backseat of the family station wagon.

"You know, Firecracker," said Father, "bringing T-Bone into the mall was the wrong thing to do."

"Boy, do I!" Alex muttered. She put an arm around T- Bone, who sat next to her. "I promise that I will never take you into a shopping mall again," she whispered. T-Bone gave her face a grateful lick.

"What you may not know," Father continued speaking to Alex, "is that, legally, your mother and I are not responsible for any of the damage that T-Bone did to the pottery shop."

"You aren't?" Alex was surprised.

"No," Father replied. "It was your fault that the dog broke the pottery because it was you who let him into the mall. But you do not have to pay for the damage because children cannot be sued in court. The law also says that parents cannot be sued for the damage caused by their children. So, according to the law, we don't have to pay for it either."

"You don't?" Alex's face brightened. Maybe her parents would not be so upset with her if they didn't have to pay for the broken dishes.

"However," Father continued, "I do not choose to live according to the world's law. I choose, instead, to live under God's law."

Alex held her breath and stared at her father. She wondered if God had some special law for children and dogs who broke pottery.

"Jesus gave us two laws to live by," Father told Alex. "One law is to love God with all of your heart and the other is to love your neighbor as yourself."

Alex nodded her head. She remembered hearing that verse before.

Father leaned across the front seat of the car and stared into Alex's eyes. "Do you think that we would be loving our neighbor if we did not pay for the dishes that our dog broke?"

"No, I guess not," answered Alex. "But you said the insurance would pay for it."

"I think insurance will pay for most of it, but not all of it."

"How much do you think it will pay for?" asked Alex.

"Well," Father rubbed his chin, "I would estimate that T-Bone did at least one thousand dollars worth of damage in that store."

"A thousand dollars!" Alex exclaimed.

"The plates that he pulled off of the table cost fifty dollars a piece."

"Brussels sprouts!" Alex cried. "Who would buy fifty-dollar plates?"

"No one with a dog like T-Bone," said Mother, joining in the conversation.

"I don't know how much the insurance will pay," Father went on, "but I think we should pay for whatever amount it does not cover. I guess that it could be several hundred dollars."

Alex bit her lip. "I guess I should help pay for it since it was my fault," she volunteered.

"Yes, I think you should," Father said.

"I have sixty dollars at home that I was saving up for a new ten-speed bicycle," Alex told her father. "You can have that."

"All right," said Father, "and I will withhold your allowance for a while."

"Okay," Alex sighed and flopped back against the seat. She would never NEVER take a dog into the mall again.

# CHAPTER 9

# Forgive Julie?

Alex had quite a surprise waiting for her when she arrived at school the next morning. A group of girls waited for her in front of the classroom door. It was the same group that had not spoken to her for the past several days. But today they wore friendly smiles.

"Hi, Alex." One of the girls stepped forward. "We're sorry that we were so mean to you."

"Yes, and we hope you will forgive us," said another.

"We made this card for you," still another girl said and handed Alex a brightly decorated, homemade card. On the inside it said, "Let's be friends again."

All of the girls had signed it.

Alex was so shocked that the only thing she could say was, "Brussels sprouts!"

The girls laughed. They turned to go into the classroom.

Alex started to follow when she heard, as if coming out of nowhere, someone whisper, "Alex! Psssst, Alex!"

Alex glanced up and down the hallway. No one was in sight.

"Alex! Over here!" hissed the voice.

Alex looked quickly to her left. The voice was coming from a side entryway. Cautiously, Alex tiptoed to the entryway and peeked around its corner.

Her eyes met the eyes of the one person she did not want to see—Julie! Alex quickly turned around and hurried back toward her classroom.

"Alex, wait! Please come back!" called Julie.

Alex stopped and stood still in the middle of the hall.

"Please, Alex, will you forgive me?" Julie pleaded.

Alex did not answer. She knew she should forgive Julie, but she was still very mad at her for becoming one of Melissa's followers. Traitor! Julie was a traitor!

Alex might have stood in the hall all morning not knowing what to do, but suddenly the late bell rang, reminding both girls that they were supposed to be in their classrooms. Alex hurried to her room. So did Julie.

"Alex, you are late!" Mrs. Hibbits told her as soon as she entered the room.

"I'm sorry," Alex apologized. She rushed to her desk.

"You know the rule, Alex," said Mrs. Hibbits, tapping her foot. "You will have to get a tardy slip from the office."

Alex stomped out of the room and down the hallway to the school office. She was doubly angry at Julie now. She had caused Alex to get her first tardy slip of the year. Julie would be lucky if Alex spoke to her again—EVER!

When Alex stepped into the office, an all-too-familiar voice said, "Hi, Alex." It was Julie! She had to get a tardy slip, too.

Alex sat down as far away from Julie as she could get to wait for her late pass. She folded her arms across her chest and refused to look in Julie's direction.

"Alex, please talk to me," Julie begged. But Alex did not. She continued to stare straight ahead. She wished the secretary would hurry up. She wanted to get away from Julie and back to class.

"What are you girls doing here?" a loud voice suddenly asked.

Alex sighed heavily. It was Mrs. Larson. Alex had hoped that the principal would not see her.

"I was late to class," Alex explained.

"So was I," said Julie.

"You girls must have been late together," Mrs. Larson guessed. "Am I right?"

Alex shrugged her shoulders. She did not know how to tell Mrs. Larson that she was not speaking to Julie.

"I guess we were sort of together," Julie volunteered in a small voice. "It was my fault that we were late."

Mrs. Larson looked at Julie and at Alex for what seemed a long time. Then, without saying a word, she pulled out a notepad and began to write.

"Julie, here is your tardy slip," Mrs. Larson said. "You may go back to class."

Mrs. Larson looked at Alex as soon as Julie had left the room. "I thought you and Julie were good friends," she said.

"Not anymore," Alex replied gruffly. "She decided to be Melissa's friend. I am not speaking to her!"

"Isn't that what the other girls did to you?" asked Mrs. Larson. "Are you going to treat Julie in the same way that they treated you?"

"That's different!" Alex replied. She took her tardy slip and left the office. She felt the principal's eyes on her back as she walked down the hall.

"Mrs. Larson can say what she wants," Alex told herself. "But I don't have to be friends with Julie if I don't want to. If she wanted to be my friend, she shouldn't have left me to be Melissa's friend."

Alex tried to forget about Julie, but all day, she was bothered by thoughts of her. Later at home, Alex tried to clear her mind of thoughts of Julie. She was in her room, finishing up her math homework when someone knocked on her door.

"Come in," Alex responded.

The door opened. Father entered the room and sat down on the bed.

Alex held her breath. Father had not yet told Alex what her punishment would be for taking T-Bone into the shopping mall.

"As you know, Firecracker," began Father, "bringing a dog into the mall is a serious offense."

Alex felt her heart sink to her toes. She would probably be grounded for a year.

"If the same situation were to happen

again, would you handle it any differently?" Father asked.

"Oh, yes," Alex answered immediately. "If I could do it all over again, I would either talk Janie or Lorraine into staying outside with T-Bone, or else have one of them call their own mother."

"Well, I'm glad to see that you learned something from it all," said Father, looking pleased.

"Oh, yeah," Alex replied. "I wish I'd never taken T-Bone into the shopping mall. I didn't mean for him to break all those dishes."

"I know you didn't intend for it to happen, Firecracker," said Father, "and intent is very important. It says in the Bible that God looks at the intentions of our hearts. That means He is as concerned with what we mean to do as with what we do."

Father smiled at Alex and continued, "So, if my heavenly Father considers the intentions of His children, then I, as a

Christian father, need to consider the intentions of my children, don't I?"

Alex nodded hopefully. Maybe she wouldn't be grounded for a year.

"Because I know your intentions were good," he said, "I'm only going to ground you for one week."

"Whew!" Alex breathed a sigh of relief. She hugged her father. "I'm glad you are a Christian father," she told him.

Father laughed and hugged her back.

After Father left the room, Alex lay on

her bed and stared at the ceiling. Her father always seemed to do the right thing. That was probably because he tried to live the way the Bible said to live. And that's what she would do, too.

Alex started to jump off the bed. But a disturbing thought made her stop. What about forgiveness? God said you needed to forgive the people who hurt you. What about Julie? If she was going to live by the Bible, shouldn't she forgive Julie?

"Brussels sprouts!" Alex muttered. She would take her bath now and think about forgiving Julie later.

Gathering her pajamas and robe together, Alex headed for the bathroom. But when she got there, she found she could not take a bath at all. Neither could anyone else. The floor of the tub was littered with a jumble of plumbing parts and tools.

"Sorry, Firecracker," Father mumbled around a screw that he held between his teeth. "You will have to use the other bathroom. I have to fix this faucet before your mother does something drastic like call a plumber."

Alex sighed and shook her head. The last time Father had "fixed" the faucet, the "hot" water had run cold and the "cold" water had run hot. She wondered what else could go wrong.

After her bath, Alex curled up in bed. She was getting ready to read a chapter in her Bible when a sudden uproar sounded outside her bedroom door.

Leaping out of bed, Alex ran to see what was happening. She met Barbara and Rudy in the hallway. They, too, had heard the noise. It was coming from the bathroom. The three children hurried to peek in the doorway.

Father stood in the tub surrounded by plumbing tools and parts. He stared up into the shower head. An exasperated look covered his face.

Mother stood beside the tub. Her hands were on her hips. She did not look very happy. "What do you mean the shower won't work?" she demanded.

"It just won't work!" Father exclaimed. "Look! Look at the faucet! It's turned on but no water is flowing out of the shower."

Barbara, Alex, and Rudy exchanged sighs. "Hey, Dad," Rudy said, "maybe if you turn the faucet off, the shower will work!"

"Very funny," Father mumbled. He fiddled a little longer with the shower head, first turning one screw and then another. Still, nothing happened.

"Well, I might as well quit for the night." Father reached for the faucet and turned the water off.

"AHHHHHH!" He screamed in surprise. Water shot out of the shower head, drenching him completely. Quickly, Father turned the faucet to what used to be the "on" position. The water stopped.

Barbara, Alex, and Rudy burst into loud laughter. But no one laughed louder than Mother.

When Alex returned to her bedroom, she heard Father say to Mother, "Okay, okay, you can call a plumber."

*Good!* Alex grinned to herself. It would be nice to have a proper shower. Then she would not have to rescue Rudy from water that was too hot.

Snuggling under the covers, Alex reached for her Bible. She opened it to the Book of Matthew and began reading where she had left off the night before: "Your heavenly Father will forgive you if you forgive those who sin against you; but if you refuse to forgive them, he will not forgive you."

"Uh oh!" Alex immediately thought of Julie. Was the Lord telling her that He wanted her to forgive Julie?

"If You want me to forgive her, Lord, I'll try," Alex prayed out loud. "But I'm still awfully mad at her. Please help me. Amen."

# CHAPTER 10

# Friends Again

A loud clinking noise woke Alex the next morning. It sounded as if someone outside her bedroom door was beating on a metal pipe with a hammer. "CLINK! CLINK! CLUNK!" went the awful noise.

Alex rolled out of bed and stumbled to the bathroom.

"Well, hello, young lady," said a strange man in answer to Alex's surprised look. The man was standing in the bathtub and knocking on the faucet with a screwdriver.

"Can't seem to get this thing loose," he mumbled. "Somebody jammed it on real tight."

Taking two steps at a time, Alex hurried down the stairs to the kitchen.

"Who's the stranger in the bathroom?" Alex asked her mother.

Father sat at the kitchen table, sipping his coffee. He groaned at Alex's question. "That is the plumber," he told her. "Your mother does not waste time."

Mother winked at Alex. "I had to get a plumber in here quickly before your father tried to fix the shower again."

Alex giggled at the look that crossed her father's face. He pretended to be very hurt by Mother's remark.

Alex was in a merry mood when she walked to school with Janie that morning. This was sure to be a good day. The shower would be fixed, she was only grounded for a week, and the girls at school were her friends again. Things were definitely looking up.

However, when Alex got to school, she found that everything was not quite as she had expected. The usual groups of girls lined the fifth- and sixth-grade hallway. But today, no one smiled at Alex or waved to her as they had yesterday. In fact, the girls in her class became very quiet when Alex passed them. Alex noticed that Melissa was back and was the center of attention.

"Oh, no," Alex whispered to Janie. "Do you think the girls are going to be mean to me again now that Melissa is back?"

At morning recess, Alex, Janie, and Lorraine suddenly found themselves surrounded by fifth-grade girls. Neither Melissa nor Crystal were among them. Julie was there but hung back from the main crowd.

"Melissa and Crystal said that you were the one that messed up the girls' bathroom," one girl accused Alex.

"What?" Alex was stunned. Surely, she hadn't heard that right.

"That's ridiculous!" Janie hollered. "Alex did not do it."

"Were you there?" a girl asked Janie.

"No, but . . . " Janie began.

"Then be quiet!"

"Melissa said that you told Mrs. Larson that she and Crystal damaged the bathroom so that they would get in trouble," the first girl said to Alex.

"Yeah, so everyone would think that Melissa and Crystal were the bad ones," added another girl.

"And so that we would all become your friends again," said a third.

Alex stared at the girls with her mouth wide open. She could hardly believe her ears. Feeling her face turn several different colors of red, Alex was just about to tell the girls that she did not care to be friends with people who believed that she damaged property and then told lies about it, when Julie suddenly pushed her way to the center of the group.

"That is the dumbest thing I ever heard!" Julie hollered. "We all know Alex. We know that she wouldn't stop up the sinks in the girls' bathroom. And we know that she doesn't tell lies either. Melissa's the one that's telling the lies. She's been lying to you all along. And you're stupid if you still listen to her!"

Julie glanced quickly at Alex. "I don't blame Alex if she never forgives any of us!" she added. And with that, Julie ran off, hurriedly brushing tears from her eyes.

A heavy silence fell upon the girls. Julie had said it all.

Alex left the group and followed Julie. She caught up with her near the softball diamond.

"Thanks for sticking up for me back there," Alex said to Julie.

"Oh, sure," Julie wiped her eyes. "I'm really sorry about everything."

"That's okay," Alex shrugged. She stuck out her hand. "Friends?" she asked.

Julie grabbed her hand and shook it. "Friends!" she agreed with a grateful smile.

At lunchtime, Alex invited Julie to join her and Janie and Lorraine at their table at the back of the cafeteria. They were all very surprised when the other fifth- grade girls began to fill up the empty spaces around the table.

"We decided that Julie was right," one girl explained to Alex.

"Yeah, we don't know why we ever listened to Melissa," said another.

"We're not going to listen to her again!" declared a third.

"We're really sorry, Alex. We hope we can all be friends again," a fourth girl said.

"Sure we can," Alex generously replied. She smiled at everybody.

"I feel a lot better now that everything's right again," one of the girls commented.

"You mean now that we're not listening to Melissa's gossip," another one pointed out.

"My mom said that gossip is like poison and whenever you listen to it, the poison spreads to you," Alex told them.

"I think she's right!" someone exclaimed. "At first it was kind of fun to listen to the gossip, but then later on, I started feeling really bad."

"Why did you stop speaking to me in the first place?" Alex asked them.

"It's really stupid," one of the girls warned.

"Tell me anyway," pleaded Alex.

"Melissa said that you take showers with your brother!" someone answered.

"What?" Alex cried.

"With Rudy?" Janie asked. She and Lorraine began to giggle.

"Why would Melissa say something like that?" Alex wondered.

"She said that when she spent the night at your house, you went into the bathroom when your brother was taking a shower. You stayed in there for a while and when you came back out, your hair was wet," the girls told Alex.

Alex frowned and tried to remember. All of a sudden, a light dawned in her eyes.

"Of course!" Alex cried. She began to giggle and giggle. Soon, she had everyone else at the table giggling.

"What's so funny?" they all finally gasped.

"It's all my dad's fault!" Alex began to explain. "See, we had this leaky shower faucet . . . "

Alex went on to tell the girls how the "hot" water ran cold and the "cold" water ran hot. She then told them how Rudy could not remember which way to turn the faucet and how he had to be "rescued" whenever he got the water too hot.

"I remember now that I had to help Rudy with the water when Melissa was at my house," Alex said.

"You mean that's what caused all this trouble?" Janie exclaimed. "How ridiculous!"

"You're right," the girls admitted.

"How about a peace offering?" someone suggested. A small package was thrown at Alex from a lunch sack.

"Sunflower seeds!" Alex chuckled.

Lorraine laughed and held out her hand. So did all the other girls. Alex shook a few seeds into the open hands. That left only a few for her but she didn't mind. She had her friends back again and the gossip was over.

Amen.